The Hand-Me-Down
Doll

BY

Steven Kroll

ILLUSTRATED BY

Dan Andreasen

Marshall Cavendish Children

Marshall Cavendish Corporation, 99 White Plains Road, Tarrytown, NY 10591
www.marshallcavendish.us/kids

Library of Congress Cataloging-in-Publication Data
Kroll, Steven.
The hand-me-down doll / by Steven Kroll ; illustrated by Dan Andreasen. —
1st ed.
p. cm.
Summary: A lonely doll without a name endures a series of terrible
misfortunes before she finally finds someone to love her.
ISBN 978-0-7614-6124-1 (hardcover) — ISBN 978-0-7614-6125-8 (ebook)
[1. Dolls—Fiction.] I. Andreasen, Dan, ill. II. Title.
PZ7.K9225Hal 2012
[E]—dc23
2011016396

The illustrations are rendered in oil paint on shellacked Bristol board.
Book design by Anahid Hamparian
Editor: Margery Cuyler

Printed in China (E)
First Marshall Cavendish edition, 2012
1 3 5 6 4 2

Marshall Cavendish
Children

For Kathleen
—S.K.

For Emily and Katrina
—D.A.

There was once

a spoiled little girl named
Glenda.

The more she had, the
more she wanted. The more
she asked for, the more she
got.

On Glenda's sixth birthday, her parents bought her a beautiful doll with long, dark curls and a velvet coat. But Glenda already had plenty of dolls. She put the new one on a shelf and forgot about her.

When her mother asked what she would name her new doll, Glenda said, "Oh, nothing."

For a long time, the doll sat on the shelf. No one held her or brushed her hair. She got very lonely. And she wanted a name.

One day, Glenda's mother discovered the doll covered in dust.

"Don't you want to play with her?" she asked.

"You can give her away if you want," said Glenda. "I don't care."

That afternoon, Farmer John stopped by to deliver eggs. Glenda's mother asked if he'd like to take the doll.

"My wife and I don't have children," Farmer John said. But he took the doll anyway and drove her home in his wagon.

Farmer John and his wife didn't have much time for a doll. John was busy farming. His wife, Sal, was busy cooking and gardening.

The doll sat looking out the window. She became even lonelier than before.

And she still didn't have a name.

In the fall, John and Sal took the doll to the county fair to decorate their vegetable stand.

The doll liked that. People noticed her and one customer said, "What a beautiful doll she is!"

Later that day, a big, gruff woman came along and shoved five dollars in John's hand.

"I'll take that pretty thing," she said.

She carried the doll away
and set her down beside some
stuffed dogs and tigers in her
ring-toss booth.

"Step right up!" the woman
announced. "A ring over
any bottle, and you win this
beautiful doll!"

The doll shuddered.
She wanted to be loved, not
gambled away.

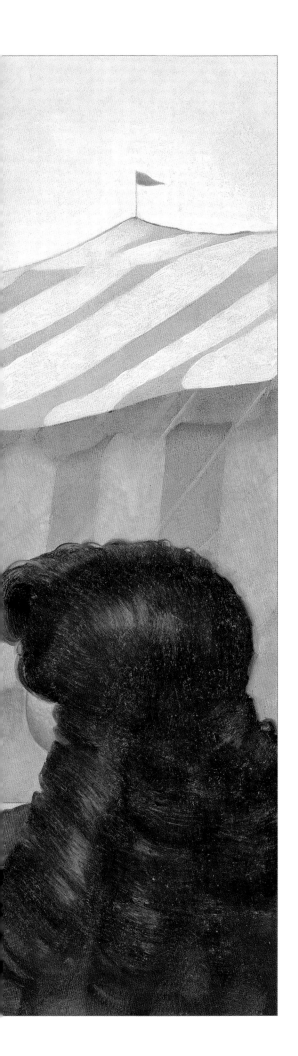

Hours passed. A man in a uniform began tossing the rings. With one ring left, he threw—and he won!

"I'll take the doll," he said. "I'll give it to my niece."

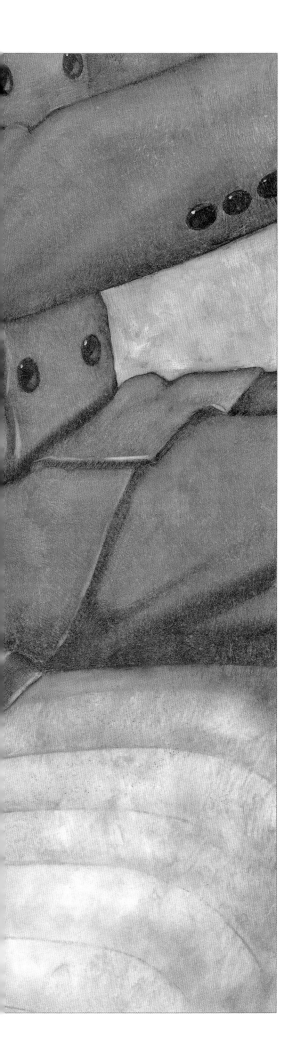

He walked to a shiny limousine, but he didn't step inside. He held the door open for an elegant couple! Then he put the doll on the front seat and drove away.

The doll wondered if she was going to a new home.

The chauffeur dropped off the man and woman and stopped at a nearby café. He greeted the manager with a shout and slapped another gentleman on the back.

The doll thought he might show her off to the people, but he didn't. He put her in a corner and left her there.

At closing time, Harry, the waiter, discovered her.

"Hey, Nell," he said to the cook, "have you seen this?"

"Keep me," the doll said to herself. *"Keep me and love me and give me a name."*

"Better leave her outside. Someone might come along and want her," said Nell.

Outside, a small, dirty-faced boy walked by. He picked up the doll and carried her off.

After awhile, they came to a neighborhood with dark, battered-looking houses. The boy set the doll down on the sidewalk.

Don't leave me, thought the doll. *It's so dirty here.*

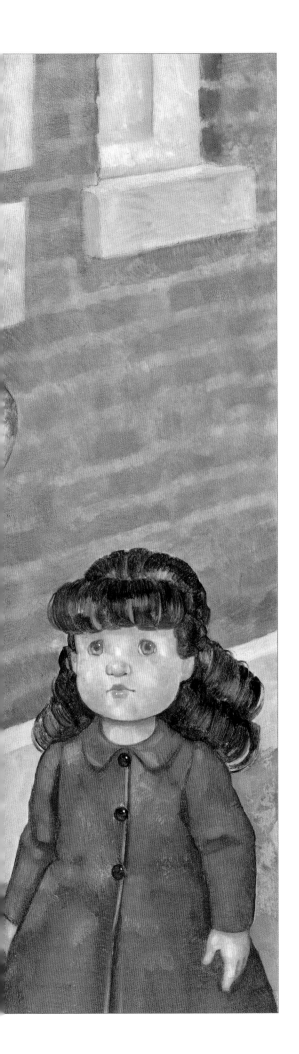

A little girl came around the corner.

"Want to buy a doll?" the boy hissed. "Cheap."

The doll's heart sank. But when she looked up, she saw a smiling, friendly face.

The little girl searched in her pockets. "Here's a nickel," she said. "It's all the money I have."

The boy snatched the coin and ran off.

The little girl carried the doll home to her parents' tiny apartment. They sat together on the worn-out couch.

"I don't have very much," the little girl said, "but having you is everything. My name is Hayley, and your name is Kaylee."

Kaylee closed her eyes and smiled. At last she was loved, and at last she had a name.